A Tooth Fairy Tale

Stephen S. Berger, D.D.S.
&
Jeanette K. Berger, R.D.A.

Illustrated by Camille Czech

FIRST EDITION

98 97 96   5 4 3 2 1

Library of Congress Cataloging-in-Publication date: June 1996.

Text and art copyright © 1996 by Stephen S. Berger, D.D.S. and

Jeanette K. Berger, R.D.A.

Illustrations in this book are by Camille Czech.

ISBN 0-9651089-9-6

Editing by Carol O'Hara

Composition and design by Caroll Shreeve

Typesetting by Nancy Elliott

Printed in Hong Kong

DEDICATION

We dedicate this book to all the health professionals who provide dental care to children. These wonderful people commit their skills and energies each day to help children grow in good health.

It is our hope that this book will be a valuable tool to help parents and health professionals alike achieve the goal of healthy children—in mind as well as body.

Stephen S. Berger, D.D.S.

Jeanette K. Berger, R.D.A.

ACKNOWLEDGMENTS

We have practiced Pediatric Dentistry in the town of Santa Rosa, California, since1975. Every parent and child has taught us something that has improved our abilities to treat and understand our young patients. We thank all of these people—past, present, and future—for their help and support.

We will forever be indebted to Camille Czech, who took our verbal suggestions for illustrations and turned them into magical works of art. Also, thanks to Carol O'Hara of Cat-Tale Press for giving us the courage to forge ahead and make this book a reality.

This acknowledgment would not be complete without a heartfelt "Thank you!" to our office staff, who come to work every day and make a difference in people's lives.

Lastly, we thank our family for being there with their unlimited love and support.

Stephen and Jeanette Berger

n a special corner of the sky, and not really that far away, lived a band of beautiful fairies. Their job was to replace the tired, worn-out stars with bright, new, shiny ones. The fairies loved their job because it was so important. They knew it would be a sad sight if the night sky was without its lovely, shimmering stars! The fairies' world rippled with laughter and joy, because they believed they would forever keep the night sky filled with bright stars made from children's baby teeth which came from Earth. These special teeth always came out just in time to make room for nice, new permanent teeth.

he tooth fairies needed many new teeth each night to replace the worn-out stars. There was an endless supply because every night, the fairies received beautiful, shiny baby teeth in all shapes and sizes. These teeth also came in many colors, from very white to shades of gray. Some had little chips in them. It didn't matter as long as the teeth were healthy. Only a healthy tooth could shine brightly enough to be a star. Once in a while, though, a tooth arrived with black spots, or even a hole in it. This made the fairies sad. Here was a child's special little tooth which could never become a star.

ne day, the tooth fairies noticed that more and more teeth were arriving with black spots and holes in them. They knew some-one must go to Earth right away to look into this problem. They chose Vesta, the kindest and wisest of all the fairies, and gave her the power to be invisible, so she could watch over the people of Earth. Her task was to find out what was happening to the children's teeth.

t wasn't long after Vesta arrived on Earth that she discovered the problem. The children had been eating far too many foods that contained sugar and not enough good, healthy foods. The little Earth people loved to eat cookies and cakes, ice cream and candy, because they tasted so good. The fairy could not understand why the children ate foods that could damage their special baby teeth. Making stars was so much more wonderful than eating lots of tasty treats!

esta, the wise fairy, also saw that the children had tiny germs on their teeth which only she could see. And these germs were a bad-mannered bunch! They were responsible for making the holes in the children's teeth. She named the germs "plaque" because in her language that meant "yucky." These bad germs loved sugar, too, and when a child ate food with sugar in it, the germs ate some sugar, too. The more sugar the children ate, the fatter the germs got. They needed homes, so the germs dug out little holes in the children's teeth to hide in. Vesta called these holes "cavities" because in her language that meant "dark caves."

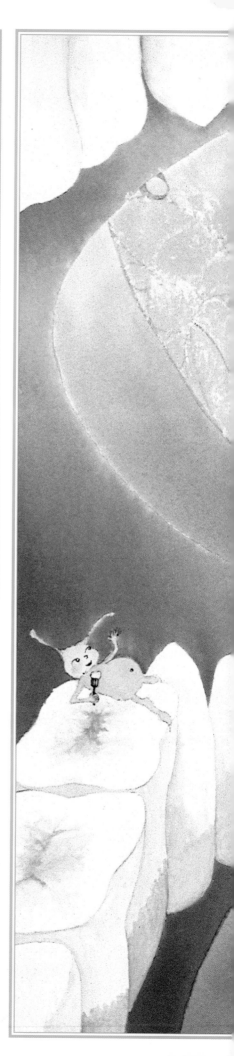

After some serious thinking, Vesta had a great idea. The children could use the same little tool on their teeth that the fairies used to polish the stars! The tool was like a little brush, so she called it a "toothbrush." She knew that the children also needed to clean between their teeth. She pulled a thread from her gown and discovered it was very good at removing the nasty old germs before they could start making cavities. She named it "dental floss." By doing these simple things, the children could keep their teeth beautiful, shiny, and healthy until their permanent teeth were ready to come in. She was sure the children would be happy to use these simple tools to keep their teeth healthy enough to become stars.

How delighted Vesta was to have thought of a way to get rid of those awful plaque germs. Now the fairies would once again have enough teeth to keep the night sky shining! But the children and their parents had to learn how to use the tools to take care of their teeth.

Hmmmmm…, she thought. *Aha!*

When the answer came to her, she laughed with joy. It had been a long time since she had laughed. She would train people to teach the children and their parents how to use a toothbrush, how to floss, and what foods were good to eat. She decided to call these people "dentists," which in her language meant "star savers."

And so that is what Vesta did. Before long, she had trained many "star savers" and taught them to call themselves "dentists." Then they began training others to be dentists, so each child would have a dentist to guide him or her in taking care of those very special teeth. The rules for healthy teeth were so simple, she knew she had found the answer to the problem. She was quite proud of herself.

hen Vesta returned to her world, all the fairies whooped with such joy, the stars shone a little brighter. Already the new teeth arriving from Earth were healthier and just right for making shiny stars. The fairies had never before seen so many stars lighting up the night sky!

The fairies decided Vesta should return to Earth to make sure there would always be enough beautiful teeth to become stars. She would inspect each tooth before she sent it home and reward the children for taking such good care of their teeth. Vesta somersaulted with happiness to learn of her new job. Because she loved the Earth children, she decided to leave them a special present in exchange for each tooth she found!

his wise and very happy tooth fairy named Vesta still lives on Earth and helps children make the stars. Don't you agree that the stars in the sky are the most beautiful, sparkling things you have ever seen?

Look closely on a clear and moonlit night. You may even find your very own tooth star!

Vesta's Suggestions to Children for Making Bright Stars

1. Brush your teeth by moving the soft brush in small circles. This helps the gums, too. Sometimes this tickles a bit.

2. Always brush <u>slowly</u> and <u>carefully</u>. Try to brush each tooth with ten small circles.

3. Let Mom, Dad, or some other grown-up help! Plaque germs can be very sneaky. Sit real still with your mouth wide open, so your helper can find all the plaque germs.

4. Use dental floss every day. A favorite place for plaque germs to hide is between your teeth where you really can't see them.

5. Eat very few foods that are sweet. Remember, plaque germs love sweet foods, and that makes them grow <u>VERY</u> fast!

6. Whenever you're thirsty, please drink water rather than juice. Ask some-one to put a slice of orange or a strawberry in your glass of water. It tastes great and looks very pretty. A good tooth-fairy rule is to drink juice or milk only with your meals or snacks, and drink water all the other times.

7. Growing children get hungry between meals. Be sure to eat snacks that are good for you, such as fresh fruit, vegetables, cheese, or popcorn.

8. If the plaque germs make cavities in your teeth, they can still be saved to become stars. The "star savers," the people we call "dentists," can use special teeth patches called "fillings." (This word means "silver stars" in fairy language.) After a good patch job, these teeth can be as bright and shiny as all the other stars.

Remember, if you follow these simple rules, your teeth may one day become bright stars for all the world to see and enjoy.

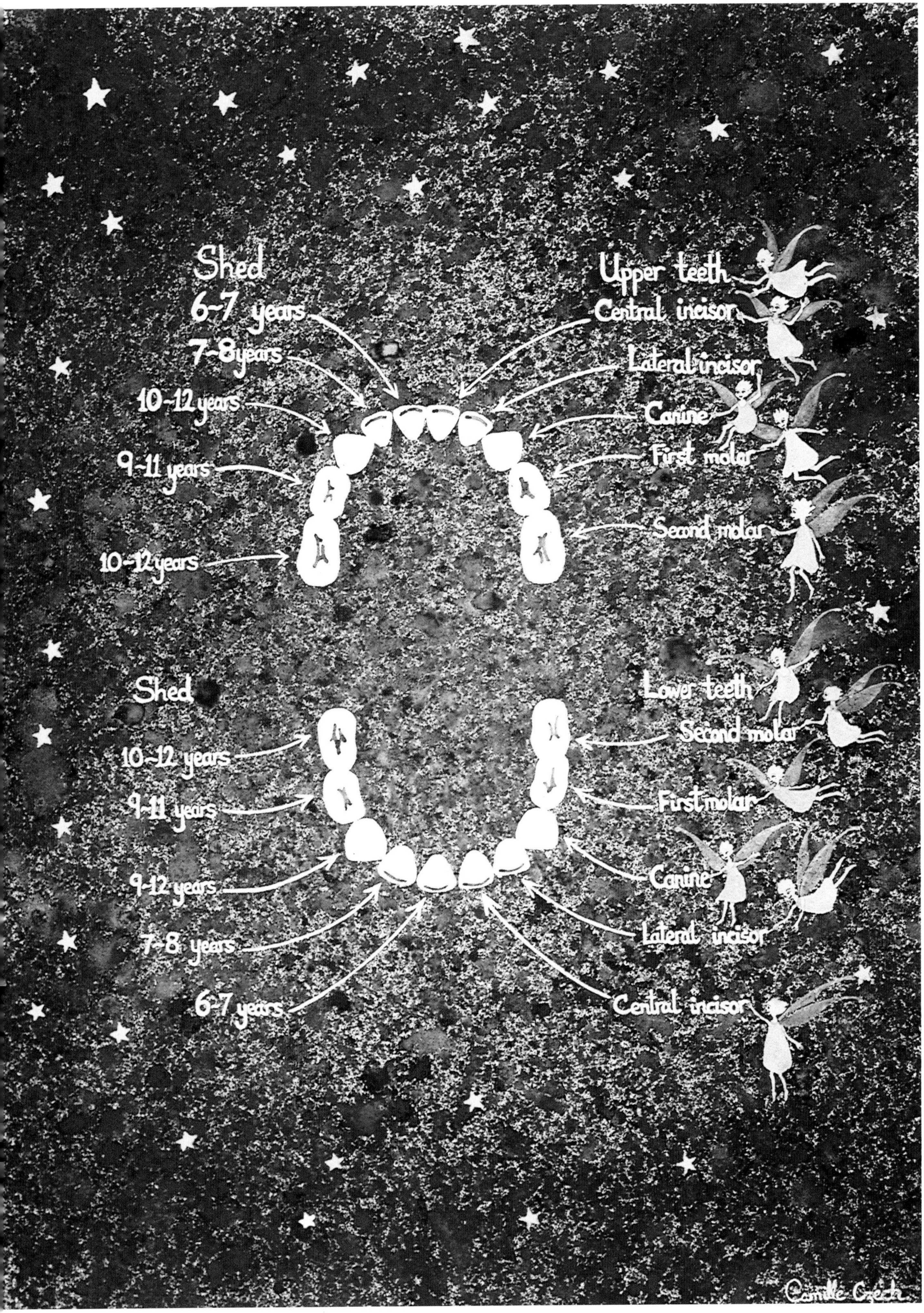
Shed
6-7 years
7-8years
10-12 years
9-11 years
10-12years
Upper teeth
Central incisor
Lateral incisor
Canine
First molar
Second molar
Shed
10-12 years
9-11 years
9-12 years
7-8 years
6-7 years
Lower teeth
Second molar
First molar
Canine
Lateral incisor
Central incisor
Camille Czech

PURPOSEFUL FANTASY

A Tooth Fairy Tale is a story for parents as well as children. Our hope in writing this book is to help parents and children have fun in achieving good oral health.

I encourage you, as parents, to elaborate and expand on this story to create enthusiasm in your children about caring for their teeth. Let your children's natural love of fantasy give them a reason to want to have healthy teeth.

Now that you have read this story to your children, take them outside on a clear night and talk about how the stars may have been formed. Share with them the idea that keeping their teeth shiny and bright will help those teeth become new stars for future skies. Reward them daily for their positive efforts with a star sticker to place on a tooth fairy poster. Tell your children that dentists are their friends, and it is their goal to keep stars in the sky.

If you encourage your children to become enthusiastic in caring for their teeth, which can include the use of our star stickers and posters, a very positive team will be formed, one that can make everyone's lives much easier . . . especially your children's.

HAPPY BRUSHING AND FLOSSING

Stephen S. Berger, D.D.S.
Jeanette K. Berger, R.D.A.

ORDER PAGE

Help for Parents from the Tooth Fairy

This book is written to encourage children to care for their teeth. If proper care is begun at an early age, children *can* grow up with decay-free teeth.

Reward systems used as positive reinforcements are the most effective way to motivate people of all ages. Thus, to encourage your children to brush and floss their teeth, we offer **Tooth Fairy posters with star stickers and tee shirts.**

Our posters can be purchased individually or in sets of five. Each is in full color and is 8.5 x 11 inches in size. All come with a set of twenty star stickers. Each time your child successfully performs the tasks of brushing and flossing, he or she earns the right to place a sticker on the poster. When all five posters have been filled—twenty stars on each one—please have your child write a personal note to the Tooth Fairy, for she loves to hear from children. Send your child's note and a check or money order for the tee shirt and any other products you wish to order to:

The Tooth Fairy
Dragonbreath Productions
122 Calistoga Road, No. 136
Santa Rosa, CA 95409
Telephone Orders: 707-539-FARY (707) 539-3279
Please allow three to four weeks for delivery.

I wish to order the following products:

Posters @ $2.00 each or $9.00 for a set of five & stickers   quantity   subtotal

1. Tooth Fairy World	page 5	_____	_____
2. Tooth Fairies Making Stars	page 7	_____	_____
3. Tooth Fairy Flossing	page 15	_____	_____
4. Tooth Fairy Beaming Tooth to the Heavens	page 23	_____	_____
5. Tooth Star Chart	page 25	_____	_____

Child's Tee Shirts @$9.95 each

Small	_____	_____
Medium	_____	_____
Large	_____	_____

𝔄 𝔗𝔬𝔬𝔱𝔥 𝔉𝔞𝔦𝔯𝔶 𝔗𝔞𝔩𝔢 **book** @ $12.95   _____   _____
(with personal tooth-loss chart for your child)

(California residents please add 7.5% sales tax)   _____
Postage/handling @$3.50 per order $3.50
Include complete mailing address with order _____

Total Amount Enclosed: _____   _____

(Customer has permission to photocopy this page)

MY VISITS TO MY DENTIST FOR REGULAR CHECK UP:

_____

_____

_____

_____

_____

_____

_____

_____

_____

comments:

ORDER PAGE

Help for Parents from the Tooth Fairy

This book is written to encourage children to care for their teeth. If proper care is begun at an early age, children *can* grow up with decay-free teeth.

Reward systems used as positive reinforcements are the most effective way to motivate people of all ages. Thus, to encourage your children to brush and floss their teeth, we offer **Tooth Fairy posters with star stickers and tee shirts.**

Our posters can be purchased individually or in sets of five. Each is in full color and is 8.5 x 11 inches in size. All come with a set of twenty star stickers. Each time your child successfully performs the tasks of brushing and flossing, he or she earns the right to place a sticker on the poster. When all five posters have been filled—twenty stars on each one—please have your child write a personal note to the Tooth Fairy, for she loves to hear from children. Send your child's note and a check or money order for the tee shirt and any other products you wish to order to:

The Tooth Fairy
Dragonbreath Productions
122 Calistoga Road, No. 136
Santa Rosa, CA 95409
Telephone Orders: 707-539-FARY (707) 539-3279
Please allow three to four weeks for delivery.

I wish to order the following products:

Posters @ $2.00 each or $9.00 for a set of five & stickers   quantity   subtotal

1. Tooth Fairy World	page 5	_____	_____
2. Tooth Fairies Making Stars	page 7	_____	_____
3. Tooth Fairy Flossing	page 15	_____	_____
4. Tooth Fairy Beaming Tooth to the Heavens	page 23	_____	_____
5. Tooth Star Chart	page 25	_____	_____

Child's Tee Shirts @ $9.95 each

Small	_____	_____
Medium	_____	_____
Large	_____	_____

𝔄 𝔗𝔬𝔬𝔱𝔥 𝔉𝔞𝔦𝔯𝔶 𝔗𝔞𝔩𝔢 **book** @ $12.95   _____   _____
(with personal tooth-loss chart for your child)

(California residents please add 7.5% sales tax)   _____
Postage/handling @ $3.50 per order $3.50
Include complete mailing address with order   _____

Total Amount Enclosed: _____   _____

(Customer has permission to photocopy this page)

Write to:

The Tooth Fairy
Dragonbreath Productions
122 Calistoga Road, No. 136
Santa Rosa, CA 95409

Telephone Orders: 707-539-FARY
                  707-539-3279

In Roman mythology, Vesta was the goddess of the hearth and symbol of the home. She particularly watched over households and family activities. Family members made offerings to her at mealtimes. In early Roman days, the importance and necessity of keeping a fire always alight became a sacred obligation for which the king was originally responsible. Later, the young daughters of the king accepted this task.